My Talks With God

iUniverse books may be ordered through booksellers or by contacting:

iUniverse
1663 Liberty Drive
Bloomington, IN 47403
www.iuniverse.com
1-800-Authors (1-800-288-4677)

Because of the dynamic nature of the Internet, any Web addresses or
links contained in this book may have changed since publication and
may no longer be valid. The views expressed in this work are solely those
of the author and do not necessarily reflect the views of the publisher,
and the publisher hereby disclaims any responsibility for them.

ISBN: 978-1-4401-7894-8 (sc)
ISBN: 978-1-4401-7895-5 (ebook)

Printed in the United States of America

iUniverse rev. date: 10/20/2009

My Talks With God

✦

Marie Wilson Hinkle

iUniverse, Inc.
New York   Bloomingt

My Talks With God

Our baby came to us

On *Oct 22*

At *8:25*

19 *32*

My birth certificae

On October 22, 1932, with my mother's help, I was delivered into the loving hands of my Grandmother Wilson, a practical nurse. My journeys through life begin in a small frame home on Wade St. in Fort Worth that was built by my daddy and grandmother.

I grew up an only child, surrounded by grandparents, aunts, and uncles who helped mold me into the person I am today.

I have learned to laugh more and worry less, that being young is beautiful, but being old is comfortable. And finally, there are two things money can't buy: true love and homegrown tomatoes. I hope to teach my children and grandchildren these truths. This is my story, as I shared it with God.

Hi God, this is Marie.

I wanted to let you know that I learned a new prayer today. My grandmother has been helping me get it just right. She says you kneel at your bed when you say it. So here goes:

> Now I lay me down to sleep
> I ask the Lord my soul to keep.
> If I should die before I wake,
> I ask the Lord my soul to take.

What do you think? Do you like it?

God, it's me again.

It was so cold last night that Abah,(that's my grandmother Wilson,) heated an iron and put it to our feet. You know of course, since you can see us, that she and I share a big bed with lots of quilts. Mother and Daddy sleep near the kitchen. I hope their feet are as warm as ours.

Wedding day for Mom and Dad

Guess what, God?

Today mother and I rode the bus downtown to see all the Christmas decorations. You should see all the toys at Leonard Brothers Department Store. I don't want to seem selfish, but I sure saw some things I liked. If you see Santa, will you tell him? We looked in the store windows, and the figures were all moving under the make believe falling snow. I'll bet you just love Christmas, especially since it's your son's birthday.

Did you miss me, God?

Did you look for me in my bed? I wasn't there.

My mother's friend, Mrs. Simpson, picks me up every year during my Christmas vacation to spend a week at her big brick home in Dallas. Do you know people in Dallas? They are very rich and have special things like big mirrors and sweet smelling powder in their bathrooms. She always gives me five dollars when she brings me home. It's funny how going away makes you glad to come back home.

Dear God, do you like snow ice cream?

It is very cold today. The sky is black as molasses, and we are trying to stay close to the gas stove in the living room. I am sitting as close to the fire as possible, playing with my paper dolls. The snow has been falling since morning, and I went out twice and came back in with red nose and wet feet.

Finally, after much begging, Grandma Wilson took her big bowl and spoon outside and shoveled up enough clean snow to make ice cream. She added sugar, milk, and vanilla, stirred it all together, and we ate it fast before it melted. To me it was better than the ice cream we eat at Scott's Drug Store. The thing I like best, God, it came from you.

I am so lucky, God.

My Mama and Papa Inman live close to us. Every Wednesday I walk from R. Vickery Elementary and spend the night with them. Last Wednesday it was freezing cold outside. We went to the corner store and bought Hawaiian Pineapple ice cream. A big fire blazed in the wood stove. We came in all frosty and snuggled next to the stove to eat our ice cream. Our front sides felt warm, but our backs were cold. What a fun time! Thank you for grandparents.

Grandma and Grandpaw Inman

God, how did you do it?

I mean, how do you make kites fly? Today my kite flew so high I could barely see it. Did you look down and see it? It is made of bright paper and has a rag tail that flows in the breeze. It stayed up most of the morning. How does that work? Do You know?

God, I have a question

Could you start over and make me a boy? I like to climb trees and play marbles. I always have skinned knees and elbows. I love to walk on stilts, swing on the grapevine trellis, and shoot rubber guns. Should girls act this way?

Dear God, who invented naps?

Summer is here and school is out. Every afternoon my Grandmother Wilson makes me lay down with her and take a nap. I'm not at all sleepy and it seems a waste of time. Anyway, she puts me on the wall side of the bed and I'm captured for the afternoon. I usually toss and turn until she says, "lay still," that makes me wiggle and squirm even more. I've tried to climb over her a time or two, when I heard her snoring, but she always catches me in the act. Finally she wakes up refreshed and I am free until tomorrow afternoon.

Why do I need to nap because Grandmother's tired? That doesn't seem fair to me.

Abah and I —downtown

God, this is Marie again,

I am lonesome today. I am playing "ball & jacks" on the front porch all by myself. I wish I had a sister to play with, but I guess some other family needed one worse than us. If you have an extra little girl with no place to go, will you send her our way?

Guess what, God'

My Grandmother Wilson and I are going to Mrs. Eula G. Bates house for a garden party. O course it's for grown ups but since she is grandmothers best friend, I am invited. Grandmother peddled on the sewing machine for weeks and produced a beautiful, long gown for the party. I didn't notice her making me one but on the day of the party, as I wiggled and squirmed,

She slipped her long silky nightgown over my head and tied it at the waist with a blue ribbon. After some pulling and draping to make the gown short enough. I was ready to go. She backed her old Dodge out of the driveway and drove to the west side of Fort Worth. I proudly sat in the front seat, beside her.

The party was in Mrs. Bates side yard, surrounded by flowerbeds and a white board fence. The ladies were all gathered and looked fancy in their long dresses. Most of them were pleasingly plump and I could tell their corsets were giving them trouble on that warm afternoon. I feel sure the neighbor kids, looking through the fence are wishing they had some of the cookies and punch. I was feeling pretty special until I became bored, spilled punch down the front of my dress and wished I were back home in my old clothes, or playing with the kids peeping through the fence,

At last, the afternoon ended and we were on our way home. Curled up in the backseat, my dressed stained and my stomach aching, I drifted off to sleep. My last conscious thought was "gosh, it's good to be a kid again."

The garden party

Dear God,

I did something bad at school today. I'm sure you already know, but I will tell you anyway. I lied to my teacher. I told her my stomach hurt, and she let me go home. I know you are disappointed with me, but to tell you the truth, by the time I walked home my stomach really did hurt. I guess what hurt most was the story I told.

Sorry, God. Do you still love me?

Guess what, God?

I looked for you tonight. Were you hidden behind the stars? My Grandmother Wilson (I call her Abah) and I slept on a mattress in the back yard. It was so hot we sprayed ourselves with the garden hose. I bet you laughed when you saw me in my underpants and Abah in her corset. It is so much fun to lie on your back, counting the stars, and listening to the night sounds. We hung a quilt on the clothesline so the morning sun wouldn't shine in our eyes.

Did you see us, God?

Are you looking, God?

Spring is almost here and I can't wait to wiggle my toes in the green grass. It's much too early, but I sneaked behind the washhouse, took off my shoes and enjoyed the cool, wet feeling of going barefoot. You won't tell will you God?

Dear God, what were you thinking?

When you made red ants, did you know they bite? There is a big red ant bed in my driveway, and I squatted down to watch the ants running up and down their ant path. I don't know where they are going, but they sure are in a hurry. I guess the babies and old ants are hid underground and the others are running for food, hoping they don't get stepped on. They seem to go about their own business unless someone disturbs their work, and then, watch out for their bite. What is their purpose, God? I can't figure it out.

Dear God, I'm worried.

My daddy didn't come home last night. We waited and waited on him to eat Sunday dinner with us, but he never arrived. Mother and Abah didn't look too worried or surprised, so I suppose they knew where he was. As it turned out he has found another lady he likes more than us. It will be lonesome without him, but he says I can visit every weekend. Although he only lives a few blocks away, it seems like miles to me. Why did he go, God?

My Dad
Archie Wilson

Don't tell, God.

I'm going to my secret hide-a-way. Guess I better tell you where it is in case I need you. I climb up the garage door and step into the old oak tree. From there it's an easy jump to the garage roof. The neat part is that the tree limbs hang on the roof and make a great hiding place. Sometimes a girl just needs her own quiet place, and this is mine. You want to come and sit beside me? You know you're always welcome.

Dear God, it's washday again.

Every Monday morning my mother and grandmother head for the washhouse, located between the grape arbor and the chicken yard. They fill the old wringer washer with hot water from the house, and away they go. It's an all day affair. The steam pours out the washhouse door, smelling like Naphtha, Rinso, and bleach. Then they fill the tubs with rinse water and start the wringer going. Every item goes through the wringer at least three times, some go round and around and have to be pulled out. Dirty clothes are pilled high on the floor. Grandmother keeps a wooden spoon to break up lumps in the soap. Then, with a mouthful of clothespins, they hang them all on the line. I love to run between the sheets that are flapping in the breeze, and they sure smell good on the bed at night. The one time I tried to help, I got my fingers caught in the wringer. That was the end of my helping for a long time.

Dear God, I've done it now.

I always try to act my best when I go to visit my dad, but today I goofed. I was roller-skating on the sidewalk when I tried to skate on one foot like I saw in the movies. Well, it didn't work for me, and I fell and broke my right arm. My dad ran out the door, saw my dangling arm and said, "For heavens sake. Let's go see Dr. Phillips." Dr. Phillips put an ether mask on me and set my arm. I got a sucker to eat, and my dad got a bill for $5.00. He said, "For heavens sake," and brought me back home. I don't think he was happy, God.

Dear God, I need help.

I'm feeling grumpy today. Every weekend I pack my small brown suitcase and walk two blocks to spend the whole time with my dad. I don't mind the walk, but the days are pretty boring, especially since his new wife, Ila, doesn't understand little girls. I have to be on my best behavior, and you know how hard that is for me.   Will you help me God?

Dear God, you did it again.

You sent a new friend to me, and she moved right next door to my dad. Her name is Bonnie. She has a dog-named Jackie. Things are really looking up. Bonnie has long black curls and wants to be my friend. She is beautiful, and doesn't mind that I have skinny legs and freckles. Maybe we can be sisters since she is an only child also. Now I look forward to the weekends. Thank you, God, for new friends

Dear God, are you excited?

Today is Sunday and things are bustling at Riverside Methodist Church. All of us kids in Mrs. Gladys' class are being baptized today. I guess they think we are a bunch of hoodlums because they seem anxious to get us sprinkled. About mid-morning we lined up and marched into the big church. We kneeled at the altar rail, and one by one we were baptized and fed crackers and juice. I think they called it wine and unleavened bread. The church people looked awfully proud. Several ladies, wearing hats and gloves, wiped tears from their eyes and hugged us. Guess this means we are real Christians and members of your family. Are you glad, God?

Dear God, I did it again.

My friend and I were playing on a seesaw when she decided to get off. Her end of the board came up and, you guessed it, my mended right arm is broken again. My dad was called. He arrived, not looking too happy. I was listening for the "For heavens sake" word, but I think I heard something worse. Anyway back to Dr. Phillips we went. This time he set it with no ether, which was a pain, but I was afraid to yell. After another $5.00 and a huge frown from my dad, we started home. Everyone hoped I had learned a lesson. The biggest lesson I learned was to write with my left hand.

Dear God, thank you for bubblegum.

    I can't wait to get to Mr. Roberts' grocery store. I don't understand why, but since World War II, all the bubble gum has disappeared. What that has to do with the war is a mystery to me. All I know is that Mr. Roberts promised to save a piece when he got a new shipment. My mother says it's not worth a penny, but that's because she never tried it. I ran to the store. I could already taste the sweet wad of gum in my mouth. I put my penny on the counter, stuck the wrapped gum in my pocket, and fled the store before anyone could see me. When I got home I immediately climbed the garage door, stepped into the oak tree and onto the roof. I settled in my special hiding place and unwrapped the gum. It was as good as I remembered it. I chewed that gum until all the flavor was gone, saved it in a glass at night, and then chewed it some more. It lasted for weeks.

Dear God, do you like chicken?

We are eating Sunday dinner at Grandma Inman's house. She always has a huge platter of fried chicken, homemade biscuits and sweet tea. My cousins and I play games and climb trees until we are so hungry we can hardly wait for dinner. The only trouble is we are low on the pecking order. The men eat first, taking their time talking and swapping stories, and then the women have their turn, eating and discussing recipes and sewing projects. Finally us kids can have the leftovers, which usually consist of chicken wings and cold biscuits. Someday we will get the chicken legs and hot biscuits and have our own stories to tell.

God, do you see us?

Bonnie and I are seated on a quilt in Sycamore Park. Her dad, Barney, was hired by Leonard Brothers Department Store to go around to all the parks and show movies in the summer. As soon as he got busy, we took off. We don't really care about the movies, but have fun playing hide and seek with the other kids. Barney told us to stay away from the bad kids. Bonnie and I looked them over, and they all looked the same to us, so we ran wild among the trees and had a great time.

Dear God, look how brave I am.

Today I am at Aunt Ada's playing with my cousins. They are all boys so naturally I try to keep up. While Aunt Ada was in the house wrestling with her old wringer washer we hatched up a plan to parachute off the garage. Charles smuggled a sheet from the house, and we tied a rope to the four corners. The boys decided it would be a good idea for me to jump first and make sure it worked. It didn't sound like a good idea to me, but I wanted to show them I was not afraid. So I gathered up the parachute, held onto the ropes and prepared to jump. I had already forgotten the lecture my dad gave me about keeping both feet on the ground. The screen door opened, Aunt Ada surveyed the situation, and yelled, "STOP." It was too late. I dropped like a rock with the bed sheet wrapped around me. My nose buried in the dirt. When I rolled out of the sheet Aunt Ada looked me over. I had no broken bones, and the boys got a paddling. As it turned out, it seemed worth it to me.

Dear God, want to go fishing?

My aunt and uncle, along with some cousins and Uncle Joe, went night fishing on the Trinity River. We jumped out of the car, grabbed our poles, slid down the steep bank, and cast our lines into the water, hoping a fish was ready to swallow our fat worms. After sitting there awhile, we became restless and looked around for something else to do. We finally decided we were wasting our time fishing and set out to explore along the river. We dropped our poles and took off. The boys and I climbed up and slid down the riverbank looking for turtles and snakes. Uncle Joe built a big fire on the bank and spread a quilt on the ground close enough to warm him as he slept. The night sounds were everywhere and shadows skipped across the water. We were having a great time when we heard a shout and a big splash. We ran back to the campsite just in time to see Uncle Joe drag himself out of the water and climb up the steep bank. He had gotten too close to the fire. His pant leg was scorched and the quilt was still burning. Everyone decided it was time to go home. Uncle Joe, smelling like smoke, was the first one in the car. We tried hiding our smiles God, but it was funny.

Dear God, I'm going on a trip.

Last night I couldn't sleep. I tried everything from saying prayers to counting sheep but nothing worked. Every time I shut my eyes I could see myself on the train headed to Houston to visit Aunt Maggie. My grandmother Wilson is sending Aunt Maggie a canary bird named Molly, and they trusted me to deliver it. I felt sick at my stomach and was already homesick when morning came, but it was too late to back out. When I got on the train with Molly I looked around for a seat by the window. Everyone seemed friendly enough, so I set the cage in the seat beside me and settled down to look out the window.

Around lunchtime I opened my lunch sack and ate the cheese sandwich and pickle. In the bottom of the sack was a big piece of chocolate cake. I licked the icing off the top and crammed the rest in my mouth, enjoying the sweet taste. Just as I felt comfortable and sleepy, Molly started singing. Everyone on the train looked in my direction. I whispered for her to be quiet, but she kept singing. I was so embarrassed I could have rung her neck. Finally she ran out of songs and everyone went to sleep again.

An hour or so later the train whistled and pulled into the Houston station. Aunt Maggie was waiting for me with open arms. We had a great time visiting, shopping, and jumping the waves in Galveston. A week later, with a lot more confidence and without the singer, I climbed aboard the train headed for home. Thank you God, for bringing me home.

Dear God,

    I have chicken pox, and I look pretty pitiful. I got so tired of staying in the house scratching that mother sent me to Aunt Othell's to spend the night. She and Uncle John have a few acres at the edge of town. I think they all felt sorry for me when they saw all my pox sores covered with Band-aids.   One of the main attractions at Aunt Othell's is their big workhorse, Old Mike. He is pretty gentle, and I have sat on his back lots of times. After supper, Uncle John lifted me up on the back of Old Mike. I was sitting there thinking how grand I looked when he turned his head, took one look at me, and headed for the barn. There was nothing I could do but hang on. The trouble was, there was nothing to hang on to. I grabbed onto his skin, hair, and finally his ears, but he never slowed down. When I looked up and saw I wasn't going to clear the barn door, I flattened myself on his back and prayed. Old Mike came to an abrupt stop inside the barn and looked around to see if I was still on. When I slid down off that horse, all my Band-aids were missing along with my pride. I wonder if Old Mike was afraid I would give him the chicken pox.

God, you won't believe this

Grandmother Inman has a milk cow in her back yard. Of course, it's behind a wood fence. I love to sit on the top rail dangling my feet and pretending I live on a farm. Twice a day Grandma sits on a stool, bucket in hand, and pulls and squeezes those faucets until she has a pail full of milk with foam on top. She let me try once and I could hardly get a dribble. God, how did you get milk in that cow and how do you get it out? It's a mystery to me.

God, do you hear them peep?

Today the mailman brought us a shipment of baby chicks. They arrived in a big cardboard box with holes in the top. Mother said that we need to keep them warm until they are old enough to go outside with the other chickens, so we put them under the cook stove in the kitchen. Those chicks peeped day and night from the time the mailman knocked on the door until they graduated to the chicken yard. We slept with cotton in our ears to muffle the sound. A few weeks later we saw them clucking and pecking with the old rooster and hens. I hope they are having a good time because mother said by fall they will end up on a platter for our Sunday dinners. Does that sound fair, God?

Dear God, you sure make interesting things.

The other night, at Grandma Inman's a bunch of us kids were chasing lightning bugs. I can't figure how you made them with a blinking taillight, but they sure are pretty. We placed them in a jar and their lights blinked all night. I'm ashamed to say that sometimes we pinched off the light and placed it on our finger like a diamond ring. Do you think that hurt? I hope not.

God, I am so excited.

Bonnie and I are at church camp in Glen Rose, which is just a couple of hours drive from home. The camp is full of Methodist kids who are all hoping for a week of adventure. Our counselors stick pretty close so we need to be extra good. Bonnie and I don't really care for all the Bible classes. To tell the truth, we had rather be out exploring and wading in the Paluxy River. My favorite time of the day is mealtime. We all line up in front of the mess hall, singing, "Here we stand like birds in the wilderness, just looking for something to eat." We sung so loud they finally ushered us in and started shoveling up the food. After our evening meal we waded across the river to go to Vespers. As I looked at the big cross on the hill, my feet slipped on the mossy rocks. Down I went. I was soaking wet so someone was assigned to go back to the cabin with me to change clothes. By the time we got back across the river and up to the big cross, the service was winding down. I did get there in time to sing "*Kum Ba Ya, my Lord, Kum Ba Ya.*"   I don't think I learned many Bible lessons but I did learn the food was good and the river cold.

Dear God, Do you like cookies?

Every week Grandmother bakes a batch of sugar cookies and puts them on top of the refrigerator, well out of my reach. The smell of those fresh baked cookies filled the house and found its way through the screen door and out to the sidewalk, where I was playing hopscotch. I knew it would not be good to get caught with my hand in the cookie jar, but sometimes I did pull the chair up and get one or two cookies if she wasn't looking. I'll show you the recipe she used. It's heavenly.

OLD FASHIONED SUGAR COOKIES

3 cups flour   1 cup soft butter
1 & 1/2 tsp. baking powder   1 slightly beaten egg
½ tsp. salt   3 tbsp. cream
1 cup sugar   1 tsp. vanilla

Sift flour, baking powder, salt, and sugar into a Mixing bowl. Cut in soft butter to fine particles. Add egg, cream and vanilla. Blend thoroughly. Chill dough. Roll on floured board to 1/8" thickness. Cut into desired shapes and bake at 400 degrees until brown.

(5 to 8 minutes) Makes 6 – 7 dozen.

Dear God, we're on our way.

My Grandmother Wilson, her husband Tom, and I are headed for Amarillo. She backed the old Dodge out of the driveway before daylight and headed west. She always drives, and he gives instructions. I sat in the backseat, looking out the window, enjoying the view. The car is loaded with suitcases, gifts for Aunt Loraine, and a picnic basket full of fried chicken and chocolate cake. At noon, we stopped at a roadside table and ate lunch.

By afternoon all I saw was lot of bare land with tumbleweeds rolling across. Finally things begin to get interesting with the appearance of Burma-Shave signs. I laughed for miles as I read these signs along the road. I wrote down my favorites:

> On curves ahead
> Remember, sonny
> That rabbit's foot
> Didn't save
> The bunny
> Burma-Shave

And this one:
> My job is keeping
> Faces clean
> And nobody knows
> De stubble I've seen
> Burma-Shave

We had a great time seeing the sand and cactus in West Texas, but I was sure glad to get home to my oak tree by the garage door.

Dear God, your going to like this.

It's Sunday night and a bunch of us kids are going to the Riverside Evangelistic Temple. We heard they had more fun than the Methodist so we are going to check it out. We sat on the back row and whispered until the characters in the illustrated sermon flowed onto the stage. The players were dressed like they just escaped from the bible and didn't know which way to run. They raised their voices in song and pranced around the stage, their robes and turbans flowed as they danced. We didn't know what to think so we just sat wide-eyed and took it in. The highlight of the program was the pastor's wife, a former belly dancer. She sang a solo that got everyone in church raising their arms in the air and shouting. Than the pastor said we were all going to Hell if we didn't come down the isle that very minute. Well we figured we were ok since we had already been sprinkled, so we sneaked out the back door and ran home. Thank you God for making us Methodists.

Dear God, do you love hobos?

My Grandma and Grandpa Inman live close to the railroad tracks, and across the Street from St. Joseph's Hospital. The trains whistle day and night and we can hear the huge engines rumbling down the tracks. The worse part is the coal smoke that settles on everything in the house. The babies in the family end up with black knees when they crawl across the floor. The best part is the Hobo's that camp along the tracks. We can see their campfires at night, smell their cooking and hear their voices. Almost every day one or two show up at the back screen door asking for a hand out. Grandma Inman never turns them down even though she doesn't have much to give. To me they look scary, dirty and smelly, but Grandma says they are God's children. You sure have lots of different looking children, don't you, God?

Dear God, I don't think you like gambling, do you?

My mother just got married, and we are moving to the Poly area of Fort Worth. Her new husband's name is Adolph, and he is almost as short as she is. They look sort of cute together, and he seems nice enough. His main problem, and it's a problem for all of us, he doesn't like to work. He likes to follow the horse races and thinks he has a formula to identify the winner even before the race. He hasn't made a dime but it keeps him busy.

I stand in front of the gas heater reading the results of that day's race to see if his formula worked. Sometimes it does, but mostly it doesn't.

Dear God, Do you like plumb jelly?

Last week my mother made several jars of plumb jelly. It flopped.   I guess she cooked it too much cause it wouldn't come out of the jar. We tried everything in the knife drawer but it's just too thick to spread.   I finally found the solution to the jelly problem.   Every day I hurry home from school, turn on the radio to *Jack Armstrong, the **all** American kid,* stick my finger in the jelly jar, dig out a wad of it, plop it in my mouth and lick my fingers.   What a treat.

Dear God, we've moved again.

Since Mother married Adolph she hoards all the money she can and always puts aside some for the insurance man, who comes to the door every month to collect. One-month mother hid five dollars in the rolled up window shade and couldn't remember where she hid it. The insurance man came back several times before she found it. Adolph decided to build a house next door to where we live. He forgot that he isn't a carpenter and we are short on money. The house still isn't finished but we ran out of money, and moved in. The other night at the supper table, mother said she had a surprise for me and it would be delivered in a few weeks. I thought I was going to get a baby sister but it turned out to be a bathtub.

The marriage lasted five years and then we moved back to Grandma Inman's, by the railroad tracks.

Dear God, are you still there?

I wouldn't admit this to anyone but you God, but going to junior high school is pretty scary. William James Junior High is filled with kids I have never seen before. Some of my friends from elementary came with me but we all seem lost in the crowded, noisy hallways. Finding our classrooms is a real trick and most of the kids are older and bigger.

Some of the girls and boys in the hallways are making eyes at each other and holding hands. We even noticed a couple steal a kiss or two. This would never go over at our elementary school but I guess we will just keep quite and see what happens next. Do you think I will find someone to kiss? It looks yucky to me.

Dear God, the stock show is in town.

My girlfriends and I are planning to go as soon as school lets out at noon. We arrived at school dressed as cowboys with jean jackets, Bull Durum tobacco sacks hanging from our pockets, and wearing old boots. We can't wait to wander down the midway, take in the sites, and look at the cute boys.

The carnival barkers tried to lure us in to see the monkey boy, elephant man, and fat lady. We stood and watched awhile, but side stepped all that and headed for the cotton candy. Walking down the midway we watched as people threw dimes in the glass cups, shot guns in the arcade, and threw baseballs at rag, dolls trying to win prizes.

Then we spotted the carnival rides and bought as many ticket as we had money. On the way home my stomach hurt and my head was spinning. I think I had too much fun, God.

Dear God, what was she thinking.

Last week, as I was going up the stairs to my next class, my friend Lola stood on the second floor landing, head stuck out the window, talking to her boyfriend, Elton. He was outside on the concrete playground. I heard her say "Elton, if I jump, will you catch me? Elton, thinking she was kidding, said "sure". Lola was rather plump and he was skinny as a rail, so naturally when she jumped, he dodged and she hit the ground. She was lucky and didn't break any bones, but that ended their courtship.

All the kids thought she was foolish, but I felt sorry for her.

This is sad, God.

Today, after lunch we were ushered into the auditorium. The seventh graders had to sit in the back section, which suited us just fine. If we were going to be griped at, we wanted to be as far away from the griper as possible. As it turned out we were given sad news. President Franklin Roosevelt had died. They said he was in his fourth term as President and had steered the country through the Great Depression. I had never paid any attention to his crutches. The principal said he came down with polio as a young man, but just kept leading our country through tough times. One of the best things he said was, "The only thing we have to fear, is fear its self." Our principal said we, should all remember April 12, 1945, as the day we lost a great leader. Almost everyone in the auditorium cried when we learned he died of a brain hemorrhage in Warm Springs, Georgia. I shed a few tears myself, even though I didn't really know him.

God, did he throw away his crutches when He came before you?

Dear God, I'm stepping out.

Tonight is the junior high prom, and I have a date. Billy Joe Hunter is a rather shy boy, but nice. He has probably been teased about his bright red hair and freckles all his life, but I think he is kind of cute. We went to the formal banquet at school. All of us girls had long dresses, and tried to be graceful and not stumble as we went up the steps. We could hardly wait for the dinner and speeches to be over so we could do our own thing. Several couples boarded a bus that took us to downtown Fort Worth. I'm sure the other passengers wondered where we had been and where we were going in our long gowns. The Hollywood theater is a block from the bus stop so we headed that way.

Billy Joe stepped right up and bought our tickets for the show. We settled down in the dark theater and waited for the movie to start. The next thing I knew he slipped his arm around my shoulders and gave me a big hug. I felt pretty grown up. Billy Joe suddenly leaped to his feet and dashed down the isle. I wondered what I said to make him leave. Maybe he was mad that I didn't hug him back. He never came back to see the movie. I found out later his nose started bleeding, and he spent the entire time in the boy's bathroom. My romantic evening was a dud. Still, he was kind of cute.

Dear God, can you believe it?

All of my friends and I from William James Junior High have finally made it to high school. It's a lot different being at Poly High around the football players, cheerleaders, and other popular kids. In the first place, we are the underdogs again, and it's a downer after being such big shots when we left junior high. Every morning as I walk through Sycamore Park and up the hill to the school. I think about the next three years and what I hope to achieve. I have never been very popular at school, so I can't imagine I will be walking around arm and arm with a football hero or turning back flips with the cheerleaders. I might try out for a part in a school play if they need someone with skinny legs and no bosoms. Anyway, here I am. I'll figure it out later.

Will you help me God?

Dear God, root for the Parrots

Most Friday nights my friend Georgia and I ride the bus to the football games at Farrington Field. We always dress in orange and black, carry the Poly banner and cheer on the Parrots. To tell the truth we don't understand very much about football but we like the players. They are cute. We sit in the stands with all our friends, listening to the band play the fight songs and help the cheerleaders by yelling as loud as we can.

Win or lose it's a fun night and we talk about it all the way home on the bus.

Dear God, I did it

I am now 16 and a working girl at H.L. Greens in downtown Fort Worth. They took one look at me and put me working behind the toy counter. My main job is to keep the bins straight and full of toys. The cash register is a challenge, but I finally got the hang of it. I plan to be the top sales person, but right now they have me walking up and down Main Street with a life size baby doll, advertising the store. I guess you have to start somewhere.

Most of the girls that work at the store are a lot older and wiser. During the break they talk about things my mother would not approve of.

Every day after lunch, I catch the bus at school and ride to work, then ride it back home at the end of the day. The first week, I made $17.02 and that's a lot of money for a girl that has none. My Dad says, "A penny saved is a penny earned." That seems like a good idea, so I will put some aside in the fruit jar under my bed

working at HL Greens

Dear God, bless Betty's parents.

I have a new friend at work, named Betty. She has three brothers and three sisters. They live in Diamond Hill. It's always exciting to be at her house and watch the commotions of her large family. Her parents are faithful members of the Church of Christ, and try to keep up with their rowdy children. Betty's mother even goes to sleep in our bed when we are out at night, so she will know what time we come home. Betty's brother, Truett embarrasses the family almost every Sunday morning when he comes weaving down their street, in front of the church, singing "My bucket's got a hole in it, can't buy no beer." I wonder how Betty's mother will ever raise those kids.

Dear God, do you see us?

I think I told you that my friend, Bonnie, has rich parents; at least it seems that way to me. On her sixteenth birthday they bought her a bright yellow Buick convertible, with red leather seats. It even had an automatic transmission. We could hardly wait to get that baby on the road. We were pretty sure we would be noticed and maybe even popular as we drove around Fort Worth with the top down. Many nights we drove down Seventh Street in front of the Hollywood and Palace movie theaters, honking and waving. I doubt her daddy knew the things we did in that yellow Buick, such as riding around in the rain, in our bathing suits, with the top down, but we sure had fun. This wonderful car was Bonnie's first love, and mine too.

The yellow buick

Dear God, please don't look.

This is our last big party before we graduate. We voted for a slumber party in the school gym. Of course it's an all-girl event. We showed up around seven with our sleeping bags, toothbrushes and the cutest pajamas we could talk our mothers into buying.

We sat on the gym floor, eating snacks and talking about our future plans until the teachers, who were unlucky enough to be chosen to watch us, fell asleep. Than the fun began. Someone suggested we prowl the dark hallways, grease the doorknobs and put molasses on the toilet seats. This sounded like a good plan so we took off up the stairs, with Vaseline and syrup. The third floor was dark as pitch, but we had our flashlights. We did our dirty work on the third floor and were finishing up on the second floor, when we heard a terrible racket. Someone was rolling the metal garbage cans down the stairs. This was not in our plans, so who else was in the dark halls besides us? My mind kept trying to say things to my body, like "Run." Our flashlights were scrolling like beacons around the hall, when we saw sneakers lined up along the wall. The boys had crashed our party. We took off running down the stairs, past the principal's office and into the gym. The noise woke up the teachers, and they were waiting for us with fire in their eyes. We jumped into our sleeping bags, covered our heads and waited for daylight. The next morning we gathered up our things, and sneaked out of the gym, hoping all would be forgiven and maybe they would blame the boys. Luckily we weren't punished but heard later that future senior slumber parties had been canceled. We felt bad and somewhat guilty. But it was all in fun.

Dear God, I messed up again.

My dad is trying to teach me to drive. Yesterday I was feeling pretty good about my abilities behind the wheel and decided to try my hand at backing the car up and down the driveway. While he was in the house reading the paper I started the engine and put it in reverse. I thought I was doing very well until I saw part of our neighbor's fence hanging on the rear view mirror. In a panic, I shifted into the forward gear and took several more pickets off Mrs. Lavender's fence. No matter how hard I tried, I just could not get off that fence. My dad hit the screen door yelling for me to stop. I did. We spent the rest of the day rebuilding the fence. To his credit, he understood, but he did keep the car locked after that day.

High school graduation

Dear God, what now?

Graduation day is finally here. I say finally, but really it seems like yesterday that I struggled to be in the school play at junior high. And wasn't it just last week that I tried out for cheerleader, and cried when I lost? Anyway, here I am, June of 1950, lined up with the rest of the graduates in a black gown with a goofy hat and orange tassel. Our family and friends are seated in the auditorium anxiously waiting for us to grab that piece of paper that says, "You made it." No more packed lunches, money for school projects, or tears of rejection. In other words, you're grown; now, get on with your life.

I think I can speak for the whole class when I say that we didn't feel that grown up but of course we wouldn't admit it to anyone. I, of course, was thrilled to get a cedar chest, a heart bracelet and other gifts for making it through twelve grades. But I'm asking you God, what now?

Dear God, you always direct my steps.

As you know, we are still living with Grandma Inman's and I am working full time at H.L. Green department store.

Last night, after work, some of us girls went to a country western dance. I wasn't sure I should be there but it turned out to be a nice, safe place, except for the table full of airman from the base at Carswell. The band played all the new country songs and we sang along while watching couples on the dance floor. A member of the band started singing "I'll Sail My Ship Alone" and the next thing I knew a guy in uniform from the Carswell table walked over and said, "Let's sail." His name was Lloyd. I'm not very good at dancing, much less sailing, but decided to give it a try. We danced the night away. At closing time he asked to take me home but I said, "No.". I did however tell him my name and where I worked.

God, will I ever see him again?

Dear God, you are full of surprises!

Across the street from where we live with Grandma Inman lives a widower named Cliff. He didn't know he was looking for another wife until he met my mother. Cliff works nights and sleeps days, so he was not easy to meet. My mother, a small, but feisty, woman set her cap for him and didn't stop until she got him. It's rumored she peeped through the window while he slept, but that may be only a rumor. Anyway before long they were courting and I was about to get three brothers.

As it turned out, Cliff, who I call Paw Paw, was the best thing that ever happened to us, and mother finally found her soul mate.

Paw and grandma Byars

Dear God, guess who came calling?

Today as I was at work behind the toy counter, I glanced up to see the good-looking guy from Carswell, you know, the one I "sailed" with at the dance. He almost didn't recognize me. It was a month ago we met, and I had changed my hairstyle and hoped I looked more mature. Anyway, there he stood. For the life of me I couldn't think of anything to say. Finally he asked to take me home after work and I quickly said, "Yes," if my mother, who was waiting for me could ride with us. He graciously said, "Sure!" and that was the beginning of our courtship.

Dear God, He's back.

Lloyd kept showing up at my door. Of course I didn't mind and Dad thought he was a great young man. He even came to visit Dad when I was out on a date with someone else. Sometimes he spent the night on the couch in our front room.

One day he showed up at Grandma Inman's while Aunt Dettie and I were trying to assemble metal lawn chairs. As he came through the gate she shouted, "If you can't cuss, don't come in." Apparently he didn't scare easily, and kept coming back again and again, driving his 1946 Ford Coupe.

After several months of dating, Lloyd presented me with an engagement ring, and although I am only eighteen, we set the date, March 3, 1951 for our wedding

Dear God, do you hear wedding bells

Mother's window peeping seems to have paid off.

She and Cliff married August 18, 1950. I have never seen her look so happy. It was a small wedding at the preacher's house with close family attending. They moved to a duplex on the south side of Fort Worth and started a new life together. Since he had no girl children, he took me on as his special project, spoiling me unmercifully, and I loved it. All this time I was planning my own wedding, only six months away.

Dear God, I'm nearing my wedding day.

My bridal shower is to be held 0n February 15th at mother's house on Boyce Street. Everyone is invited and I am really excited.

I saved my money and bought a royal blue suit to be married in and a cute hat, with flowers on top, to go with it. (They are still in layaway). Mother arranged for the flowers and cake for the reception, which will be at my Dad's house.

The wedding will be in the prayer chapel at Riverside Methodist Church, where I was baptized. It looks like everything is arranged, so why am I so nervous?

Dear God, I hear wedding bells.

I woke up this morning and wondered, "Do I really want to do this?" My next thought was, no backing out after I say, "I do."

The preacher is ready, the flowers are here, the cake has a bride and groom on top, the groom is anxious (I hope), and the family is excited about the wedding. I have the rest of the day to be a girl, and then I'll be a married lady.

We arrived at the church around six o'clock, walked up the wooden stairs to the prayer chapel and waited outside the door. Lloyd really looked handsome in his uniform, and I felt pretty dressed up myself.

The guests were seated and the organ was playing "*The Indian Love Call.*" The organ knocked as the organist played, but we were too nervous to notice.

The pastor, a young assistant was conducting his first wedding and shaking like a leaf. We bravely marched up the short aisle and stood in front of him. He recited all the wedding vows, making us promise to honor and obey. (I crossed my fingers on the obey part.) Finally he got to the good part, looked at me and said, "Do you Margaret take Leroy as your wedded husband?" I didn't know anyone named Leroy, much less Margaret, but I was taught not to argue with the clergy, so I said, "Yes." I could hear the guests behind us snickering and whispering, but I wanted him to get on with it. Finally he pronounced Margaret and Leroy man and wife and we kissed. Just as we were escaping back down the wooden steps, I heard Dad say, "If I had known that kissing was going on, I would have loaded my shotgun."

Dear God, It's March 3rd, 1951 and I'm a married lady.

It doesn't seem possible, but sure enough, I have a wedding band on my finger.

We drove a few blocks to my dad's house for the reception. The cake and flowers are beautiful and the family is all gathered with happy smiles on their faces. In a few days my mother's parents, the Inman's, will celebrate 50 years, so that makes the day even more special

I can't help but wonder what the future holds as I offer a piece of cake to my new husband, and I'm sure he wonders the same thing. We haven't really thought about the "richer or poorer," part of the vows, nor are we concerned about the "sickness or health." We are thinking about our honeymoon night in the garage apartment behind my Dad's house.

That night as we slept, Dad's dog, Wiggles, ate the flowers off my hat. If our wedding day is any indication of our future life together, it's going to be a fun and interesting life.

Someday, yes someday, when I am an old woman I will write-------

"The rest of the story." Because in the end, the only thing we own is our story.